toys

pyjamas

bed

dressing gown

slippers

bath

soap

parcels

cards

box

bread

honey

juice

apron

cookery book

tin

oven

presents

bicycle

engine

wheels

train

cake

candles

trees

flowers

cow

scarecrow

birds

butterflies

squirrels

spoons

napkins

balloons

party hats

sandwiches

cake

book

cards

bridge

horse

fence

tractor

tracks

toothbrush

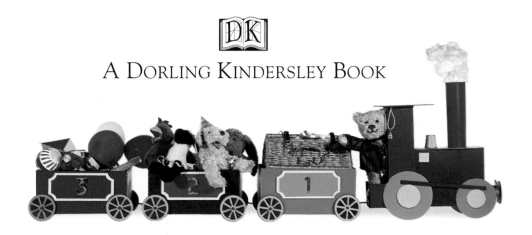

A DORLING KINDERSLEY BOOK

Senior Art Editor Penny Britchfield
Senior Editor Sheila Hanly
Assistant Editor Finbar Hawkins
Production Josie Alabaster

Photography Dave King
Additional photography Paul Bricknell and Alex Wilson

First published in Great Britain in 1994
by Dorling Kindersley Limited,
9 Henrietta Street, London WC2E 8PS

8 10 9 7

Visit us on the World Wide Web at
http://www.dk.com

A CIP catalogue record for this book is
available from the British Library

ISBN 0-7513-5072-9

Colour reproduction by Colourscan
Printed in Italy

Acknowledgements
Dorling Kindersley would like to thank the following manufacturers
for permission to photograph copyright material:
The Manhattan Toy Company for "Antique Rabbit"
Folkmanis Inc. for "Furry Folk" hen puppet
Ty Inc. for "Toffee" the dog
Vera Small Designs for the lamb

Dorling Kindersley would also like to thank the following people
for their help in producing this book:
Jonathan Buckley, Hugh Sandys, Barbara Owen

 Can you find the
little bear in each scene?

P.B. Bear's
Birthday Party

Lee Davis

DK

Dorling Kindersley
London · New York · Stuttgart

M eet P.B. Bear.

The P. stands for Pyjama, because his

are his favourite clothes.

time is his favourite time of day.

Can you guess what the B. stands for?

One morning, woke up early. This was

one day he didn't want to stay in .

He put on his  and and went into

the  room. He filled the basin with water and

washed his face with . Then he dried his

fur with a  and brushed it with a .

Finally he looked at himself in the .

"Happy birthday, ," he said to himself.

He put on his best , , and ,

and went downstairs.

There was a knock at the  .

"Mail for Mr  ," said the postman, and he gave

two  , three  , and one

huge  that was bigger than all the rest.

"I wonder what's in the  ," said .

He wanted to open it straight away, but he hadn't had

breakfast yet. So he went to the kitchen and ate some

 and  , and drank some .

Just as he was finishing, there was another knock at the .

There was his friend, Dermott the  , with a

 with a big  on it.

ma B. Bear
rietta St.
nt Garden
don
C2

AMA B. BEAR
HENRIET
GARDE

P.B.Bear

Mr Pyjama B. Bear
9 Henrietta St.
Covent Garden
London
WC2

11

"Happy birthday, ," said .

"Do you know what's in the big ?"

"I don't know," said .

"It's almost big enough for a , or

a , or a ," said .

"It's so big, it might even be an !"

"We'll have to wait until I've opened it to find

out. But I've got some baking to do first.

Will you help me?" asked .

put on an and opened

a cookery  .

He put butter and sugar into a bowl and Dermott added the eggs and the flour. Then they took turns stirring the mixture with a spoon until it was smooth.

poured the mixture into a

and put it in the .

Just then there was another loud knock at the .

Look who had come to visit.

Russell the  brought a

wrapped in paper.

Hilda the brought a

wrapped in paper.

And Lucy the brought a

wrapped in paper.

"Happy birthday, !" they all shouted

as they handed him their .

"Thank you very much, everyone," said .

"What's in the big ?" asked .

"Maybe it's a ," said .

"Or a  ," said .

"I know! It's a ," said .

"Why don't we open it and find out?" said .

got a pair of and

cut the .

He opened the .

What do you think he saw?

Inside the 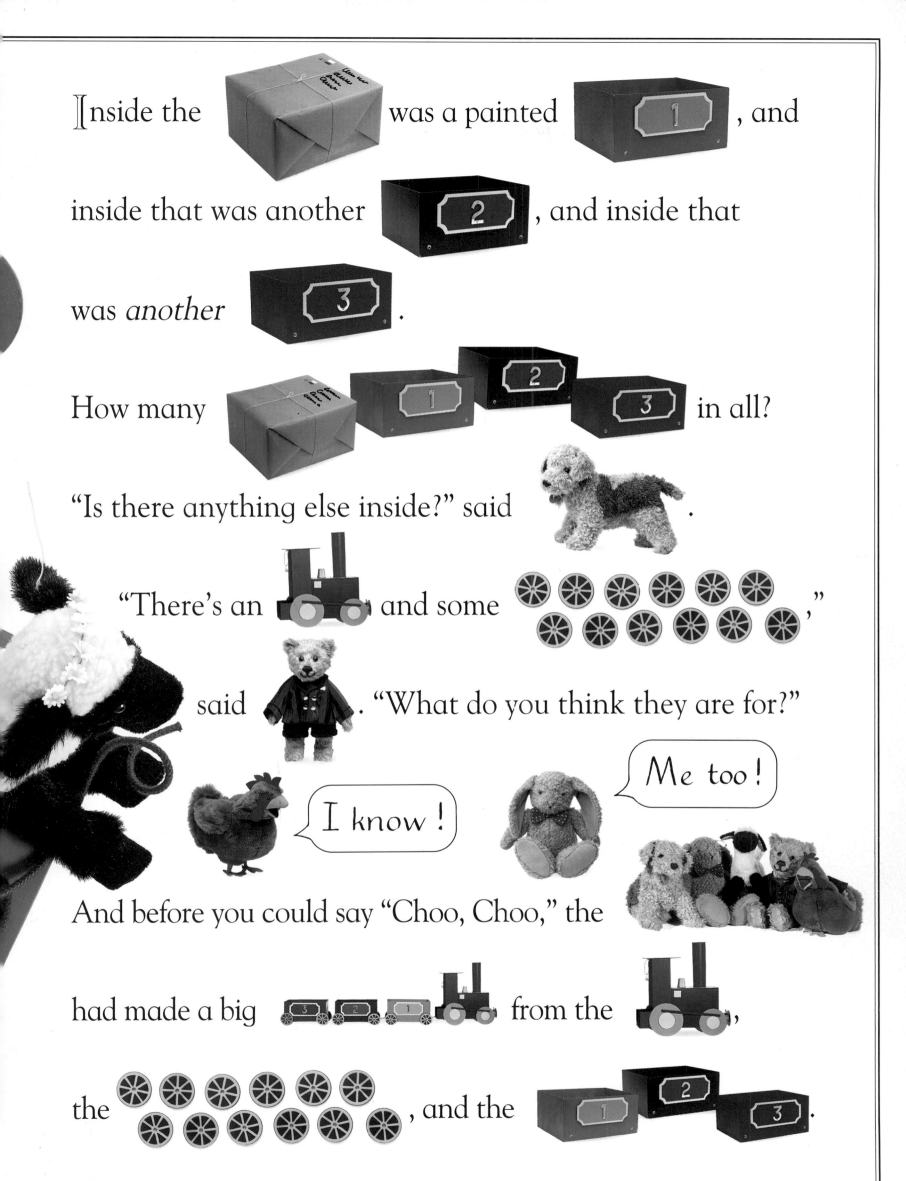 was a painted 1 , and inside that was another 2 , and inside that was *another* 3 .

How many in all?

"Is there anything else inside?" said .

"There's an and some ," said . "What do you think they are for?"

I know !

Me too!

And before you could say "Choo, Choo," the had made a big 3 2 1 from the ,

the , and the 1 2 3 .

"Let's go on a picnic!" said  . He

out of the . Then

while and the other

Can you see all the things

They put the in the

and the and

"All aboard!" they shouted as they

At last they were ready to leave.

rushed back to the kitchen to take the

put icing and ||||| on the

filled the 🧺 .

they put in the 🧺 ?

first car of the 🚂 ,

📧 in the third car.

climbed into the second car.

"Off we go!" said 🐕 .

19

The  left and went out into

. There were and and

"Ready or not,

9 10

8

7

6

5

4

3

2

1

climbed out of the they climbed and they stopped and "Finally it stopped

"Boo! Happy birthday,"

closed his eyes and started to count.

the other

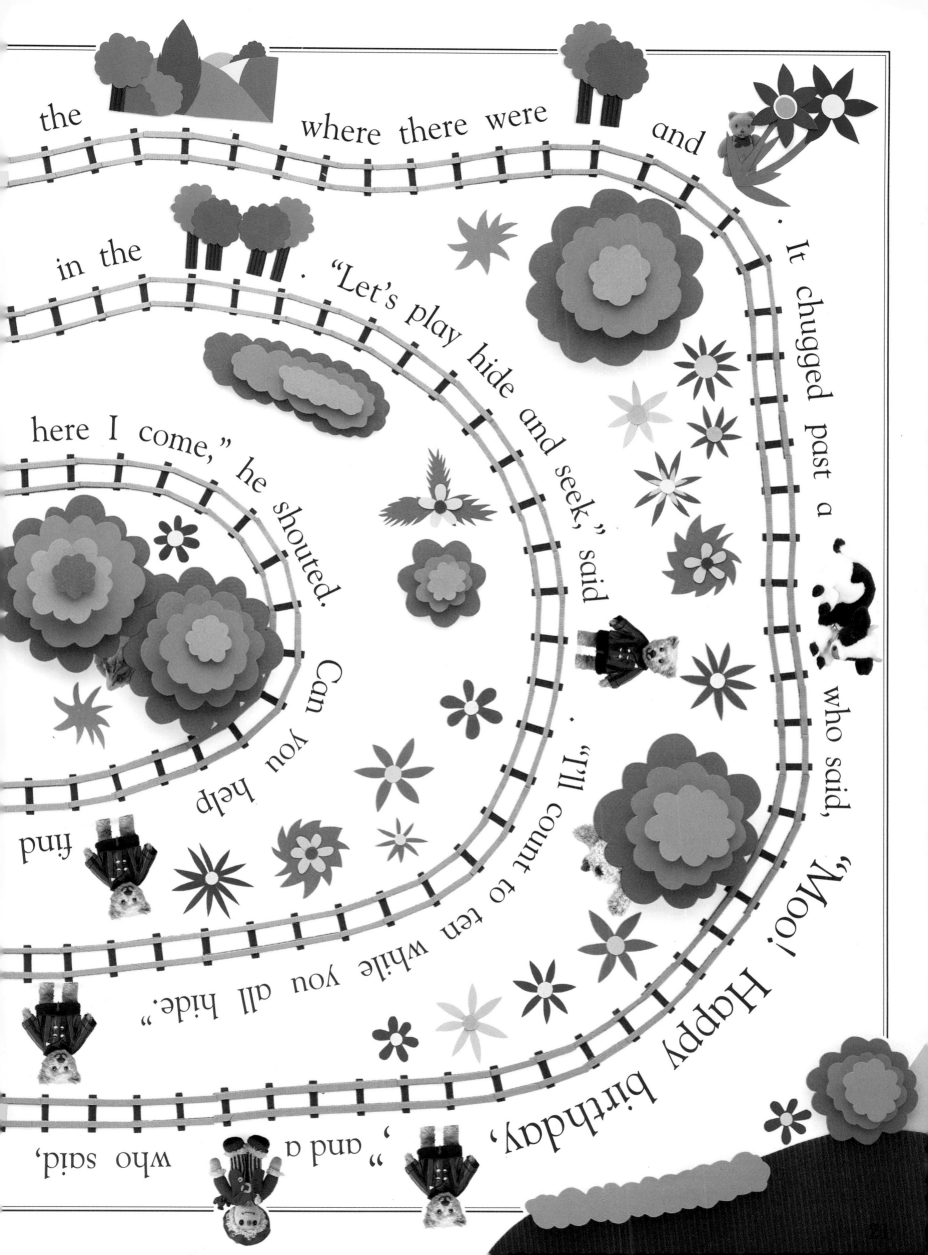

the

where there were

and

. It chugged past a

who said,

"Moo! Happy birthday,"

in the

.

"Let's play hide and seek," said

here I come," he shouted. Can you help

find

"I'll count to ten while you all hide."

," and a

who said,

"Let's eat," said .

"Good idea!" said the other . They took

the  out and spread it on the ground.

Then they put out the , the ,

the , the , the , and the .

They blew up the  and put on .

"Let's sing happy birthday to ," said

as he lit the  on the  and started to sing.

Can you work out how old is today?

The  ate the tasty and drank

the . Then they all had a piece of .

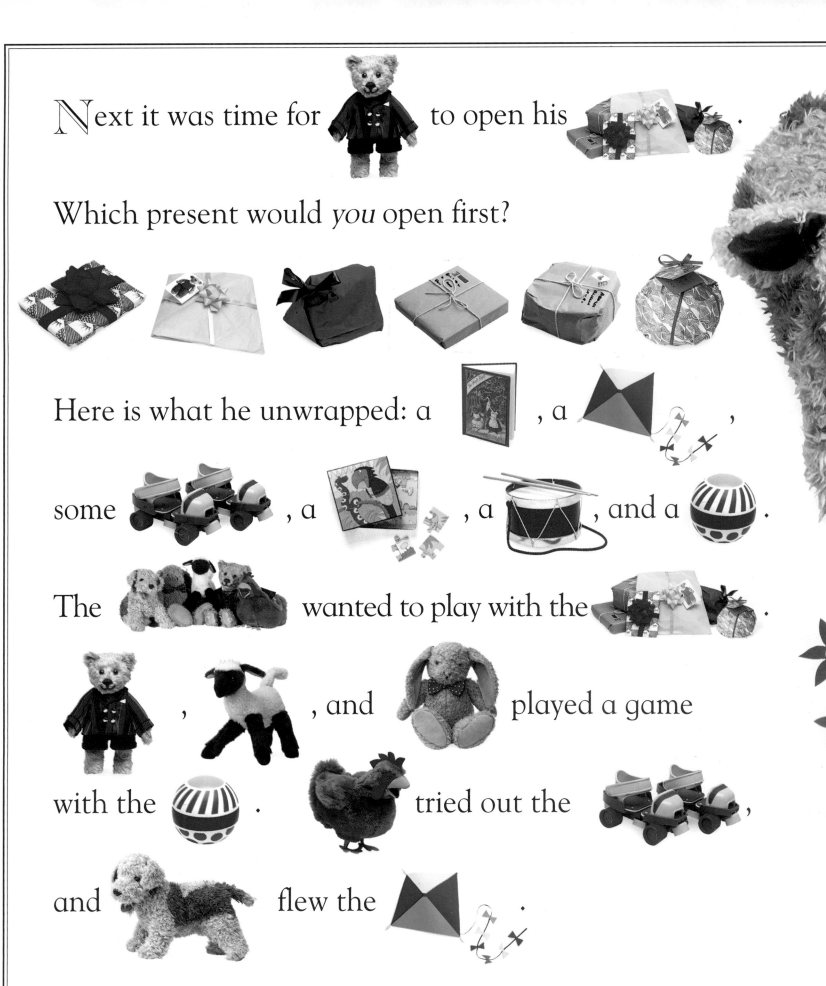

Next it was time for ⬛ to open his 🎁.

Which present would *you* open first?

Here is what he unwrapped: a 📖, a 🪁,

some 🛼, a 🧩, a 🥁, and a ⚽.

The 🧸 wanted to play with the 🎁.

🧸, 🐑, and 🐰 played a game

with the ⚽. 🐓 tried out the 🛼,

and 🐕 flew the 🪁.

It was time to go home. They packed up the and the and in the third car.

"All aboard!"

The crossed a and went past a

for a that was driving very slowly across the .

and all the

26

put it in the first car of the  . They put

Only some crumbs were left behind for the .

shouted .

who raced along the beside them. They had to stop

Soon the was back in

said good-bye.

When he got home,  was very tired.

He took off his ⬛ , 🧥 , and 🩳 ,

and put on his 👕 , his favourite clothes.

He brushed his teeth with his 🪥 .

Which of his 🧸 do you think

he took to 🛏️ with him?

Goodnight, 🧸 !

P.B. Bear   Dermott   Russell   Lucy   Hilda

towel   brush   mirror   shorts   jacket   bow tie   door

present   bow   tiger   zebra   kangaroo   elephant

car   fire engine   scissors   string   boxes

cake   basket   presents   town   country

cloth   plates   cups   knives   forks

kite   roller skates   jigsaw puzzle   drum   ball   presents